THE SURPRISE PARTY

PAT HUTCHINS

THE SURPRISE PARTY

RED FOX

Other Picture Books by Pat Hutchins

Changes, Changes
Clocks and More Clocks
Don't Forget the Bacon!
The Doorbell Rang
Good-Night Owl!
Happy Birthday, Sam
King Henry's Palace
One-Eyed Jake
One Hunter
Rosie's Walk
The Silver Christmas Tree
Titch
Tom and Sam
The Very Worst Monster
The Wind Blew
You'll Soon Grow into Them, Titch
Tidy Titch
Where's the Baby?

A Red Fox Book. Published by Random House Children's Books,
20 Vauxhall Bridge Road, London SW1V 2SA.

First published by The Macmillan Company, New York 1969. First
published in Great Britain by The Bodley Head Children's Books
1970. Red Fox edition 1993. Copyright © Pat Hutchins 1969.

Pat Hutchins has asserted her right to be identified as the
author and illustrator of this work.

RANDOM HOUSE UK Limited Reg. No. 954009
ISBN 0 09 920721 4

for MORGAN

"I'm having a party tomorrow," whispered Rabbit.
"It's a surprise."

"Rabbit is hoeing the parsley tomorrow," whispered Owl.
"It's a surprise."

"Rabbit is going to sea tomorrow," whispered Squirrel.

"It's a surprise."

"Rabbit is climbing a tree tomorrow," whispered Duck.
"It's a surprise."

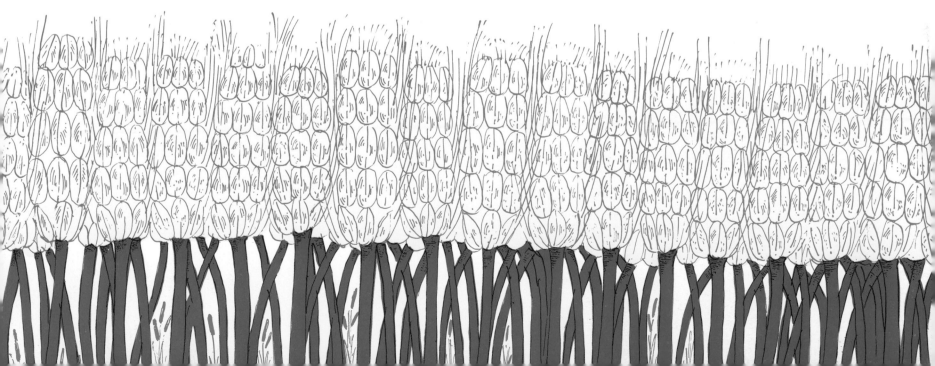

"Rabbit is riding a flea tomorrow," whispered Mouse.
"It's a surprise."

"Rabbit is raiding the poultry tomorrow," whispered Fox.
"It's a surprise."

"Reading poetry?" said Frog to himself.
"His own, I suppose. How dull."

The next day Rabbit went to see Frog.

"Come with me, Frog," he said.

"I have a surprise for you."

"No, thank you," said Frog.

"I know your poetry. It puts me to sleep."

And he hopped away.

So Rabbit went to see Fox.
"Come with me, Fox," he said.
"I have a surprise for you."

"No, thank you," said Fox.
"I don't want you raiding the poultry.
I'll get the blame."
And he ran off.

So Rabbit went to see Mouse.

"Come with me, Mouse," he said.

"I have a surprise for you."

"No, thank you," said Mouse.
"A rabbit riding a flea?
Even I am too big for that."
And Mouse scampered away.

So Rabbit went to see Duck.
"Come with me, Duck," he said.
"I have a surprise for you."

"No, thank you," said Duck.
"Squirrel told me you were climbing a tree.
Really, you're too old for that sort of thing."
And Duck waddled off.

So Rabbit went to see Squirrel.

"Come with me, Squirrel," he said.

"I have a surprise for you."

"No, thank you," said Squirrel.
"I know you're going to sea,
but good-byes make me sad."
And Squirrel ran up the tree.

So Rabbit went to see Owl.

"Owl," he said, "I don't know what YOU think I'm doing, but

I'M HAVING A PARTY."

And this time everyone heard clearly.

"A party!" they shouted. "Why didn't you say so?"
"A party! How nice!"

And it was a nice party.
And such a surprise.